Sex EDUCATION

WRITTEN BY A Black Woman

Sex Talk and Activities For You And Your Partner

Author- Adrian Pnut Steward

SEX EDUCATION WRITTEN BY A BLACK WOMAN

Sex Talks and Activities for You and Your Partner

Copyright © 2021 by Adrian Pnut Steward

Printed in The United States of America

ADRIAN.PNUT

CONTENTS

The IntroDicksion To

Sex-Education

"She was so moist from the back I could barely keep it in. Her cum dripped down the inside of her thigh while her moans made my penis enlarged to gently caress the inside of her vagina walls."

Now that I have your attention, WELCOME!!! Well, I'm going to get straight to it! This book is about SEX. Not just about how to have sex or why your girl isn't wet anymore when you've been banging her back out for two hours straight in the same position, or why your dude doesn't seem excited anymore while having sex because you use the same up and down motions...but we are actually going to learn a thing or three. Ok, maybe not much for some of you freaks, but we are going to talk about sex issues that we don't talk much about while doing some activities. You've made it past my intro, so let's get into the good stuff.

Let's go over some phrases you will see throughout this book. Like Dick for instance. That word is so bold. Let's say it slow. DIIIIIIICK... Well, that just heated things up. I like the word dick. It's that tender piece of meat that hangs between the legs of a King. Cock is the word the white man used in flicks when I was growing up. "Ewww that's right, suck this cock." Didn't like how it was pronounced then and I still don't like how it's pronounced now, so I like to call it Cock Glock. Just added some thug behind it! Pussy is another bold word! I love the word pussy. I like to put pussy and bitch together. Pussy bitch! Vagina sounds like something dry so I don't call it that. In some parts of this book, you will see me call it "Noonsie." Noonsie is just the wet word for Vagina or Pussy or Pussy Bitch! Before learning how to please your mate, you have to understand the body parts. The two main parts in this book are the Noonsie and Cock Glock. Of course, we will talk about other areas that will bring sexual satisfaction but one must learn more about the privates!

If you are reading this with your partner for the first time, congratulations! We should be comfortable with the body parts that we are here to talk about. This book will make you more comfortable to have a perfect sex talk with your partner. Hell, whoever partner you're with! Discussing how you feel about sex, or different positions or certain things you are unaware of could help to improve your relationship or just your sex life. In my opinion, it's best to have talked about sex with your partner before engaging in sexual activities and not during. The activities in this book will make it easier for you to express yourself and have fun while doing it. There is a lesson here for everybody, even my most experienced people.

Now that we are all on the same accord let's move on. I like to call myself a sex educator. No, I didn't graduate with a degree in sexology, but I took plenty of sex education classes, made it my own business to take an extra concentration in sex-sociology while in college and I participated in a lot of hands-on experiences, 'if you know what I mean'. I've had help from listening to millions of my colleague's stories and plenty of group chat talk about what we wish would happen during sex that we never speak of. Having those conversations could be awkward. Am I complaining about what I want or am I just speaking the truth on what could please me? Either way, finding an easier way to bring the topic up and talk about it makes everything much better.

I was about 8 years old when I got my first glimpse of what sex was. I saw my first flick! I didn't really have a clue about what sex was. I just remembered seeing a white female bouncing on the bed with a white man while making humming noises. At that time, I didn't know why her grown-ass was so excited about bouncing on a bed and trying to out-sing somebody! I stumbled across this video while I was at home. I just happened to turn on the TV and there it was. I'm still not sure who was watching it at the time, but hopefully, they ended their night well. I remember the channel like I was just watching it yesterday, Channel 597-Direct TV! I remembered that channel for a long time! I never had the courage to go watch it again until one day at school, one of the boys in my class brought a torn picture from a magazine that showed a female laying on the bed with her hand on her Noonsie! I could tell by the way her mouth was formed; she was making the same sound like the white lady from the flick. That made me curious!

During the weekends, I was the only one up early. This particular weekend I got up extra early. I turned the volume all the way down and typed in channel 597. Behold, there it was. This time it was a black lady and a black man staring at each other. It wasn't what I was looking for but I watched until the man was standing over the female as if she was on her knees praying to him. Didn't know what that was about but I turned it off because it had to be the wrong channel! No one was jumping on the bed this time. Where was the fun?

Of course, a couple of years later, I grew to understand everything that happened in that video and plenty more! Now we are here! Porn, as some folks may call it, could be very educational. It's a chance to look at how other people tackle sex. You have to find which ones best suit you. It all depends on if you are watching alone to get aroused or if you are watching with your partner to peep new moves. Watching flicks prior to having sex also gives that extra push. For the female, you will begin to pulse wetness on the inside of your Noonsie preparing for entrance. For the male, the Cock Glock will start itching to wake up to its full attention. Watching flicks with your partner could add some more intimacy to your relationship. You get to experience what other couples' sex lives look like. I usually get a good laugh out of porn especially the ones with a story connected to it. Laughing and learning new moves equals a good time!

Some sites to keep in mind when searching for flicks includes, Pornhub.com, XXNX.com, Twitter- it is plenty there, Xvideos.com, and to purchase flicks you could try onlyfans.com.

Dick-cussion- Talk about your views on flicks with your mate or in a group. Do you watch them? Have you made one? Would you make one?

Dick-Cussion

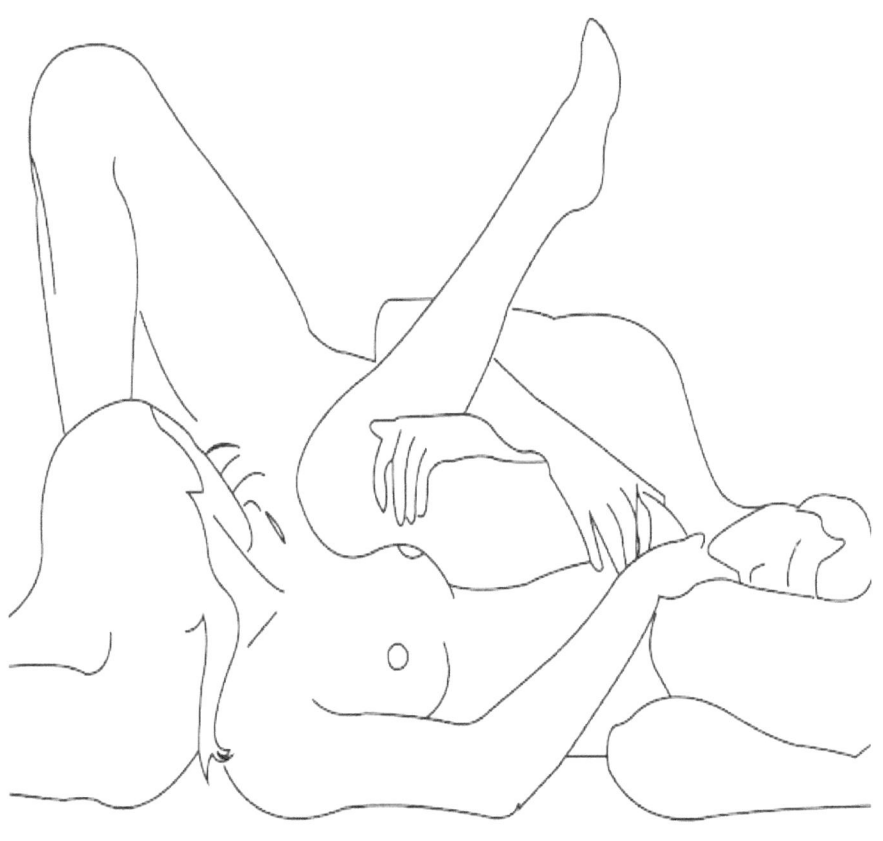

"Let's Open Up to Each Other"

Miss Pretty

Pussy

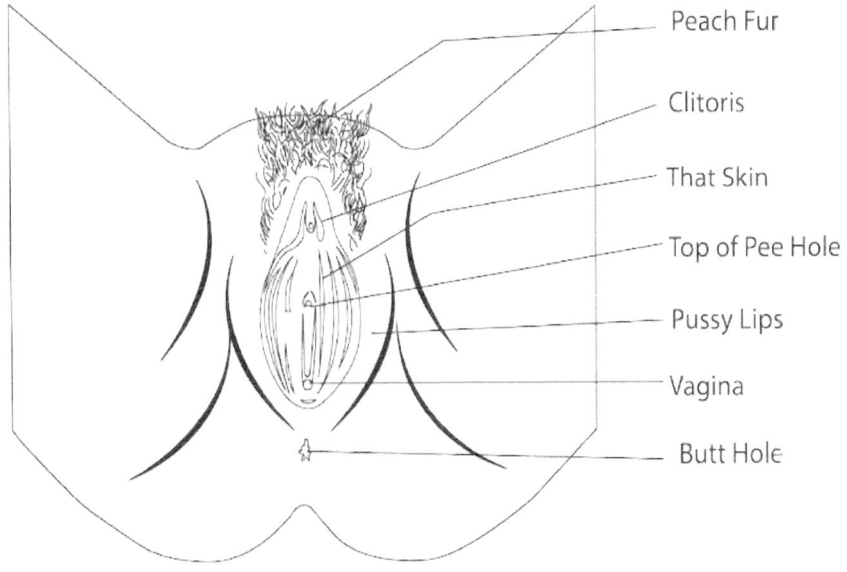

Noonsie/Pussy

If this is your first time seeing one of these, we have a long way to go. What you see here. is one of the richest gold mines ever to be discovered. This piece of art could cost someone their life, their family, even their bank account. It holds so much value. This alone could destroy a nation of wholesome men and women all due to a treasures dark sinkhole. Pussy holders, please know your worth!!

This picture is an outline of the Noonsie. Let's go over the different parts. As you could see from the image, the most important parts are labeled. Peach Fur isn't available on all Noonsies. It's what I like to call the accessory. Some women don't have Peach Fur. I've seen many porn videos where the females have nothing there, a thin strip of hair, or a 1960 fro. Believe it or not, no matter what it was, it did not stop intercourse.

When I was in college, a guy told me to never shave it bald because he still wanted to feel the friction on his skin. He also mentioned that only babies should be bald and I was a grown woman. Fast forward two years later, okay maybe two months later, Noonsie was introduced to another guy who preferred her to be bald! See, it all depends on the partner. But like I mentioned before in both cases, it did not stop the intercourse. Pussy holders, please know your worth!!

Moving right along to the clitoris. If you don't learn anything about the female private part just remember the clit! You wouldn't need to know anything else, honestly. The clitoris is actually longer than what we see by just looking at the picture. The tip of the clitoris only peeks out. The rest of it hides inside waiting for someone or something to come along and wack it until she's satisfied. Please, please, please, remember this piece of gold has more than 8000 nerves! 8000! So, this means that if you caress this gentle enough, in any kind of way, you should be creating pleasure. Please don't act like you're mad! Women hate when you play with the clit too hard. It only takes a light, love movement. Once the clit begins to enlarge it becomes easier to find a motion that works. We will talk about the clit in this book a lot, but for now, just remember it is the most important part of the female's body.

Next is That Skin. Not so much to talk about but it's the skin that hangs around the clit. The size differs from person to person. Sometimes it's nice to nibble on this part just to get the clit more moist. A real eater knows this. Down to the Top of Pee Hole. If you're nasty, then that might be a nice spot for you! The Pussy Lips are like the protector of the clit. They hold everything in place. After you peel the lips back you will enter a Holy Ghost land of saved royalties. Nibble on those also. The Vagina is the base of everything. It's right above the butthole. The butthole could be viewed as a treasured piece as well if you are into using that part during sexual activities. I know women who go as far as having sex in the butthole or as far as just a friendly finger when hitting it from the back. This is also another popular spot for some tongue action. Again, it is all about preference!

Dick-Cussion: Ladies, go over the chart with your partner prior to having sex and talk about your favorite part of the Noonsie. Let your partner know what you don't like and parts of the Noonsie that you are willing to experiment with.

Dick-Cussion

Cock Glock

King

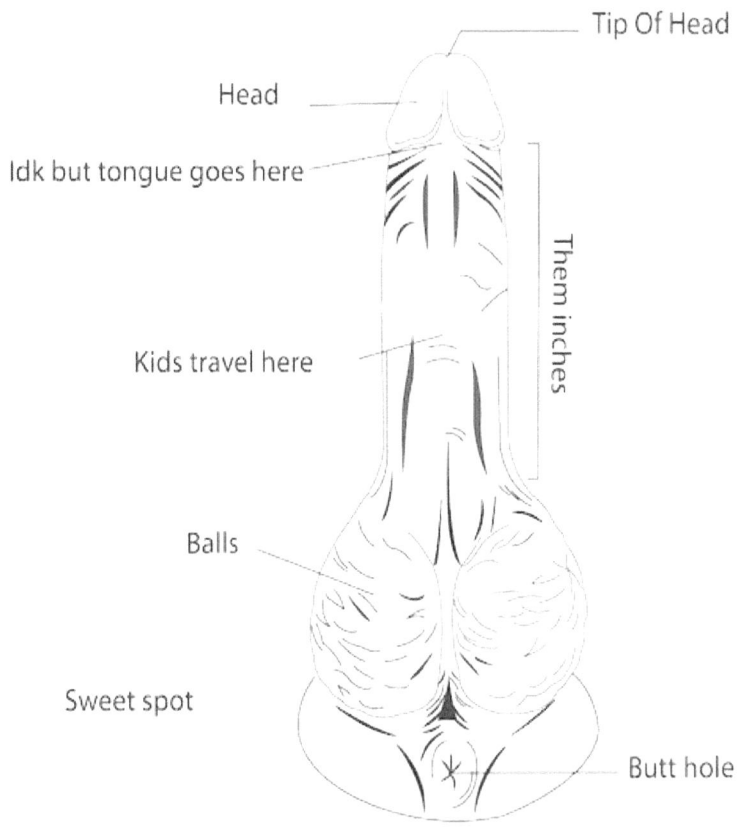

Tip Of Head

Head

Idk but tongue goes here

Them inches

Kids travel here

Balls

Sweet spot

Butt hole

Cock Glock/Dick

21

Yessss Sirr! This piece of poison is also referred to as the Dick! The sweetest piece of meat a man can carry! Just like the Noonsie, a good Cock Glock could change some lives. It's always nice to watch something grow into something amazing right before your eyes. Now that's magic! First, we are going to go over the important parts of the Dick and then we will go into the different sizes.

Take a look at the Cock Glock picture. Starting at the very top we have the tip of the head. This is the highest point on a Cock Glock. We can also call this the pee hole. If there is ever a tangy taste at the tip, my advice is to go no further. Some guys don't wait until that last bit of pee drops down into the toilet. Y'all have to remember to shake it off too! Newhoo, moving on! Next up is the Head. The Head is like the jacket of the Cock Glock. The top protector of it all. It's a little bit meatier than the rest of the penis and softer too. In a way, you could compare it to the lips of the Noonsie. A different type of feel from the rest of it. This too is an important piece of the meat. A lot of feeling sits at the top. You could be creative with the head but we will get more into that later. The spot right under the head is unknown! I don't know the name of that area but it is also important. The tongue goes there, that's all I know! This very small area is sensitive to the male. It's like the mystery piece of the entire thing. Depending on the size of the head, this spot should be visual for you to get to. It's the perfect size for a tongue to lay and caress the area.

Now, to them inches! This zone could be thick or slim. It also shows you how much length you have to play with. As you may know, every dude is different. I'll discuss that later on. This area is also the area I like to describe as the tunnel or the area that the kids travel through. All of this area needs attention too but it depends on your partner rather, or not if you need to stay just in this zone or not. Taking your tongue from the tip of the head all the way down the tunnel where the kids travel through gives guys a little excitement. It's a great warm-up for anything. Doing this motion before giving oral or before having sex is always a good choice. You can travel your tongue all the way down to the balls. The balls are very unique because of the different textures you will come across. As with any sexual act, some people just don't like it. I've learned that the balls are a part of the body that some guys love for you to play with and then you have some guys who really don't care if you touch them at all. The balls are to be gently sucked on or slowly gobbled on. This motion will feel better to the guy if you hum while doing it. Humming will send vibrations back up to the head of the Cock Glock allowing you to work everything at once.

This next spot is for those of you who aren't afraid to keep going down. The sweet spot is that secret zone. Playing with this spot surprises the guy because it is so much work to get to it and half of them don't even know it exists until someone goes and wakes that area up! Don't get this part confused with the booty hole. The booty hole is lower and has a totally different feel. Both of these areas should be discussed. You def don't want to surprise the wrong guy by going too far. Don't let the booty hole fool you though. Some fellas love this area as well. You are really working some magic when you are able to entertain the lower zones while jacking off the rest of the dick. No worries with practice anything is possible.

DICK-Cussion: Fellas, go over to the chart with your partner prior to having sex and talk about your favorite part of the Cock Glock. Let your partner know what you don't like and parts of the Cock Glock that you are willing to experiment with.

Dick-Cussion

Hard

A Story by
Nathan

We sat in the car for a minute reminiscing on the good night we just had. At one point, I didn't even know what she was saying because I was so caught up with the way her laughs reminded me of a girl I use to fuck in college. At that moment, I wondered if Shelby Green still rode dick like a porn star. It was probably the worst time to think about that freak Shelby when I had a beautiful, wholesome, queen right in my face. I snuck and took a peek at my pants to make sure that they were still big enough to not show how my penis had started to grow on the inside. I just smiled at her hoping I didn't make it obvious.

The sounds of 6lack played through the speakers and the moon was at a perfect height for me to give some head but she sat there quietly staring out the window. I placed my hand on her leg. She was wearing some black tights but I could tell that she had buttermilk thighs underneath. I wanted to lick them!

She looked at me with a familiar look in her eyes. A look I had seen in the eyes of Shelby Green. I knew what she wanted. I traveled my hands up towards the inside of her thigh. She had somewhat of a stomach but I didn't mind a lil extra meat.

She placed her hand on top of mine, so I stopped. I didn't want to move too fast. As I started to move my hand away from her thigh, she grabbed my hand firmly. The way she grabbed my hand I knew she could jack the hell out of some dick. To my surprise, she moved my hand closer to her pussy. The warm feel between her legs gave off a beach vibe. I wanted to be laid out in the sun with her ass in my face. That was my green light. Could it be that she too wanted the same thing? I pulled back the rim of her tights and her breathing became more intense. Her legs began to slowly open, thereby giving me more room to place my hand inside of her tights. Behold! She didn't even have underwear on. I grabbed her pussy lips to see how big they were. Already, I could feel the wet glaciers spillover from the inside of her vagina. I went in. I took my index finger to roam around. She scouted up a little bit and her body demanded me to roam some more. How long was she waiting for this? I took two fingers and in a circular motion, I began to knock heads with her clit. I could hear the soft moans along with the finger action, both going at a steady beat. It wasn't enough. I wanted to see what her insides felt like. In and out, in and out I went with two of my favorite fingers. She was no longer quiet with her sounds. I could tell she was enjoying my hand play by the way she grabbed my arm as if it was a handlebar. She started to help by moving my arm back and forth. With each motion, I could feel more and more glaciers.

I sped up a little bit because I could hear her moans get a little lower. I pulled my fingers out of her hole and started back on the clit. There it was; the moans I had wanted to hear. These were the climax moans. She grabbed my arm tighter and began to squirm around in the seat. Her breathing became shorter as her chest moved up and down and her head tilted back. It had happened. I had fingered her pussy until she had enough. I pulled out my fingers and we both watched the white cum slide down to my knuckles. The face she gave me was that of an angel. The same face Shelby used to give me after sucking on her breast. It was a sign of pleasure.

She rubbed my stomach. Yep, I had extra meat too. I looked down at my pants giving her the green light to go further down because he was ready! She was taking too long to get the hint though, so I unbuckled my pants to show my briefs. My dick jumped from the eagerness of wanting to be felt. She pulled back the rim of my briefs and grabbed my dick with force just like I imagined. She then asked me, "Is it on the hard?"

D Size Chart

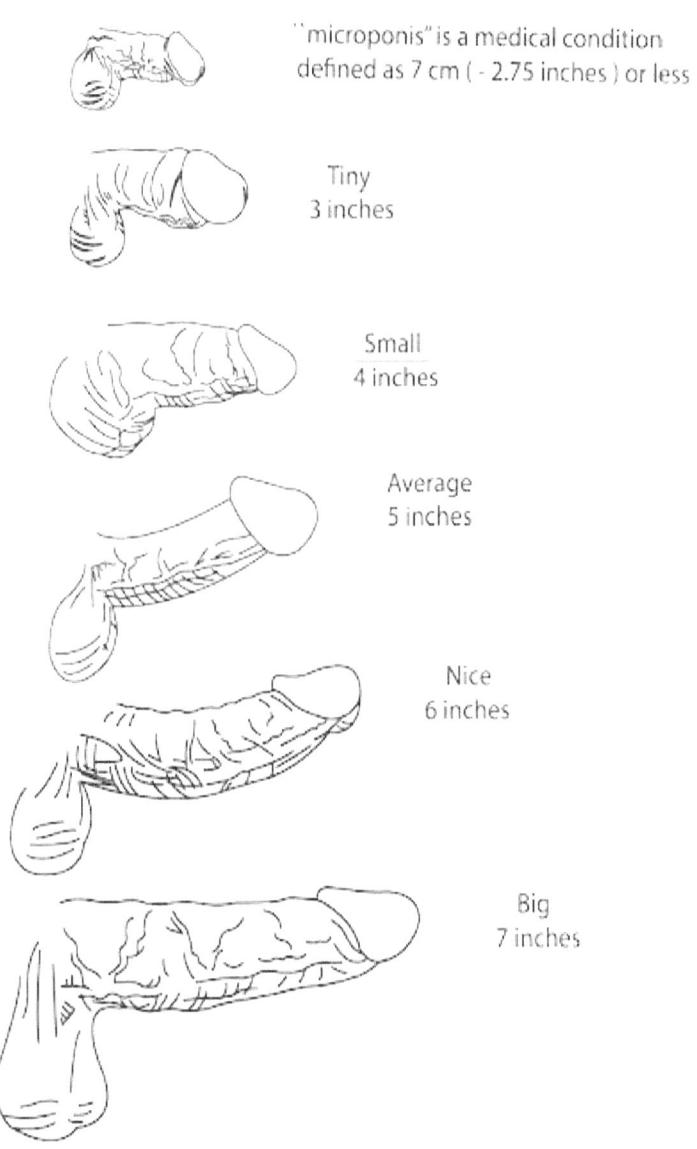

"microponis" is a medical condition
defined as 7 cm (- 2.75 inches) or less

Tiny
3 inches

Small
4 inches

Average
5 inches

Nice
6 inches

Big
7 inches

Size Matters

Should men talk about their penis size before sex? I've only experienced one guy telling me about his size prior to showing it. I believe it was his way of letting me know not to have my hopes up for a big penis when the time came. It was the smallest thing I have ever seen. I was able to grab and hold it with just one hand. For all the fellas with this size package, please don't get discouraged. I never said it didn't get the job done.

Let's take a look at the chart. This isn't every size Glock out there but these are some of the main sizes. Up first is the micropenis. This is a medical condition. It grows to become a little bit bigger than what you were born with. The sad thing is, it's not their fault. If you do not see yourself with this sized penis, then please do not lead them on. Ask them if they give head instead. If you are already in love, then oh well! It's not all about the size they have or is it?

The next size is the tiny size. It's not a medical condition but it is rather tiny for some grown folk's sex. This size usually comes out in the dark after the foreplay to ensure the size does not get in the way. By the time they pull it out. It is too late and too dark so you wouldn't even know until it was the actual time for work. The small size Cock Glock appears to be a tad bit longer than the tiny one. Both sizes still come below the recommended size. Just remember all sizes could and still get play. It is all about marketing. A friend of mine told me that her best orgasm came from a dude with a small size penis and he told her that he was sure to give her an orgasm. She glorified his penis like it was the steak at the Last Supper. That goes to show that some prefer the smaller ones.

The "average size" is good enough. This is the standard size for males. Not too small or too big. This size we don't talk about much because it is what we expect for a guy to be holding. If we talk about the meat size to our friends, it is usually because it was small or because it was big. If it is average and good, we tend to use the phrase, "He wasn't the biggest but it was good." The "nice size" is what a lot of dudes claim but some of them are barely pushing the average size. I don't know where the six-inch dick started from but they were correct. I could remember at one point in time, dudes were really taking a ruler and measuring their dicks. Maybe it was just the freaks I was dealing with that did this, but I didn't mind receiving a dick pic every now and then.

"Big size," is 7inches or bigger. The big guns. Very different in size from the average size. Have you ever heard of the saying, "Big Dick Energy?" These guys have the right to have big dick energy only if they know what they are doing with it. It's nothing like having a big dick in front of you or in you in this case and it's not good. I hear all the time how a guy had a nice size but didn't know what to do with it. The cockiness of having a big one could interfere with actually getting the job done. So, in some cases, the phrase, "It's not the size of the boat but the motion of the ocean," could somewhat be true. Of course, not everyone is going to agree with me because some of y'all love big dicks regardless. Like I mention throughout these lessons, It's all about what your preference may be!

Pussy-Talk: Let's have a small talk! Have a talk with your girlfriends not including your partner on the size of meat you prefer. Tell stories on the different sizes you've had, heard about, or will like to try.

Pussy Talk

_____
_____
_____
_____
_____
_____
_____
_____
_____
_____
_____
_____
_____
_____
_____
_____
_____
_____
_____
_____
_____
_____
_____
_____
_____
_____
_____

Titty City

A Bang

A Story by

Megan

Waking up to a tongue on my nipple was what I've been missing out on my whole life. A good lick of the nipple to start my day. We have been dating for about two months. Last night was our first time having sex and today was our first morning together. I wanted to go out with a bang. The plan was for me to wake up before him, rub on his chest and enjoy the sunrise before I had to get up and leave, but I guess the tequila from last night was still holding on. Nonetheless, I laid there while he took his succulent tongue and cleaned around my areola. We slept naked, so his penis poking my side ensured I had some work to do. I enjoyed the moment for a few seconds before making my move. Like I mentioned, I wanted to make the morning special for him. Especially after last night with him doing all the work. After he caressed and licked on my nipple, it was time for me to return the favor.

Becoming pleased with his slow tongue motion, I began to hold my breast to make it easier for him to enjoy them. The more I gripped my breast and moaned, the more tongue action I got. I couldn't let him get the best of me without even starting on him. I grabbed his face to perform mouth to mouth action. I kissed him like my nipple went missing down his throat and my tongue was going to get it. That nasty stuff early in the morning! I reached for his penis while sucking on his bottom lip. The head was all I could feel without leaning all the way over. So, I played with what I could. He enjoyed it. We got into a lying position that was comfortable enough for both of us.

This was the first time I was finally able to please him, and at the same time, he pleased me. He was such a pleaser and didn't take interest in asking me to do anything extra. This was new for him. I was grabbing and slowly stroking the top of his head with the warm part of my hand. I wasn't even jacking it yet. Just slow motion at the top of his head. I wanted to do more. I wanted him to feel as good as I did the entire night. He continued to suck on my nipple with such elegance. I stopped him and brought his mouth back to mine. My other hand was still on the top of his penis. I let my mouth get real watery from his kisses and then took my hand and let the slob drop right into my palm. He looked at me like I was becoming someone else. I stared back to make the moment more magical. As I said, I wanted this morning to be the best. I took that same hand and placed it back around the tip of his head. The moisture from my slob made it much easier to caress and start a slow stroke down to the middle of his core. I still stared him in his face. His mouth opened, wanting to taste the inside of my mouth again. I kissed him. With every kiss I gave, I jacked him at the same time. He laughed at my creativeness. It was time for me to do more.

I pushed him over on his back. His dick was sticking straight up in the air like a stop sign and I was prepared to get a ticket! I started by placing my titty in his mouth. I watched him suck on it. After he closed his eyes, I pulled it out and began to use my breast to travel down to his neck, then to his chest, and then down to his stomach. He watched me every step of the way. I was really pleasing him this time and he was loving every minute of it. I got face to face with his penis. I kissed it on the side and then kissed the other side before placing the top all the way in my mouth. He made a noise that I had never heard before. I was doing it! I was pleasing him.

It only took three real sucks for me to get my groove back. I hadn't sucked dick in about four months but from the way I was deep throating it, you couldn't even tell. He got comfortable and grabbed my hair while I went to work. I was pretty sure that he was about to nut. I wanted him to nut on my breast so I stopped sucking and started jacking to ensure I would get a good aim. It was time to finish our first overnight stay with a bang. I stroke and stroke until he uttered the words that he was about to nut. To my surprise, he nutted on both of my nipples and went back to sucking. I guess it's safe to say he loves sucking titties.

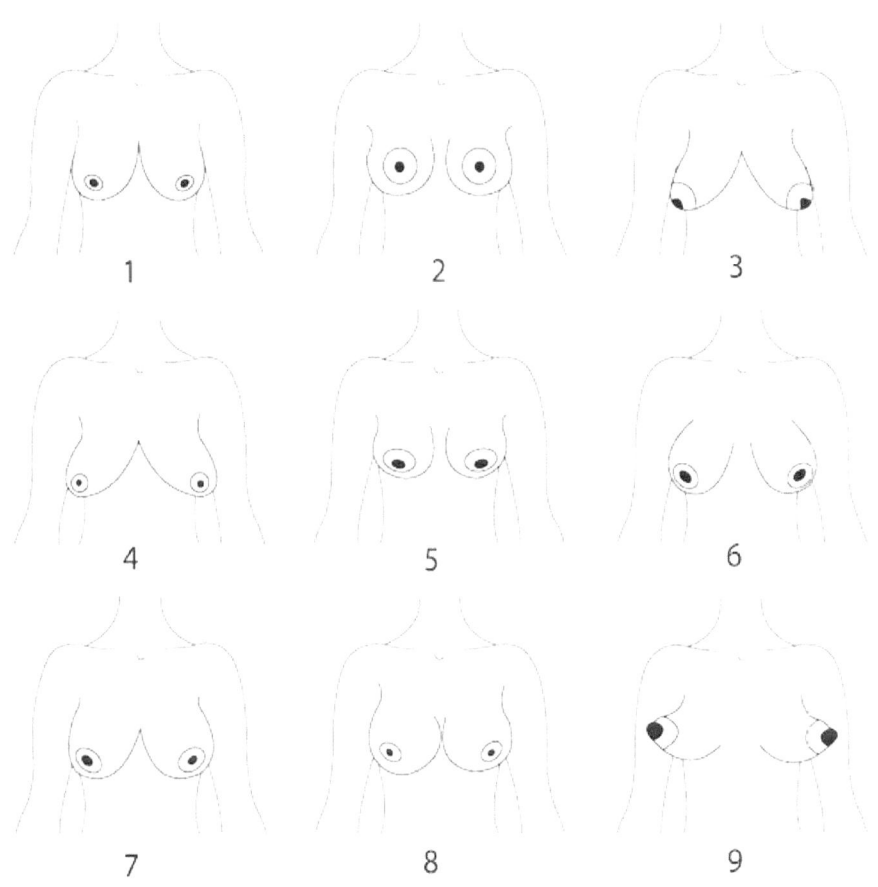

"Titty Me Down"

I have a love-hate relationship with breasts. I hate having them sometimes but I love when a guy finds it in their heart to show my titties some love. Breasts tend to have wear and tear because the longer you have them the longer they wear you out! Just like Cock Glocks, breasts come in all different sizes and shapes. From big breast to small breast, from big nipple to small nipple, from big areola to small areola, there is plenty to see and choose from. The good thing about titties is being able to wear a bra to give you the look you want or having surgery to keep the look you want. When it comes to sex and the time to take that bra off comes, the real deal is revealed.

Let's take a look at the "Titty Me Down" chart. The chart shows nine different options you could come across. All of them are perfect! Unless your bra is musty from wearing it ten days in a row, someone will find a way to suck on them, hold them, or lay on them. Not all men are titty lovers though. Some don't get the excitement of having titties jump around in their face while the lady is on top riding. Sucking titties could please both the giver and receiver. I've read how some women have experienced orgasms from getting their titties sucked. This is a blessing.

In a lot of discussions, I've been told that for some women, having their titties sucked doesn't turn them on. Believe it or not, some women don't feel it or the pleasure isn't there. In these cases, men just don't know how to suck titties, and/or these women just rather skip the sucking breast part and go straight to war! For those doing the sucking, there are different approaches we can take.

There are plenty of ways to suck on titties. You could place the boob or boobs in your mouth, depending on how big they are, and suck. By sucking on the breast gently and caressing the part of the breast that couldn't fit all the way in your mouth with your hand is a good starting point. Next, picture the nipple as the clit we talked about earlier. Play with your tongue around the nipple giving it different motions. Move your tongue fast and then change it up to slow. Incorporate some tongue flicks and soft nipple bites. Always listen out for the moans. Whatever action makes her moan the loudest, refer back to doing that motion. The main thing to remember is to take care of the breasts. Titties aren't the best place to play rough. Treat them like newborn babies.

Titties could also please the male. It is called "Titty Fuck." This is the action of having a Cock Glock in between the titties with an up and down motion as if he was stroking inside of a Noonsie. The size of the breast will make a difference in doing this. The female will push their breast together creating a small slot in between the titties. It is a good idea to lubricate this slot. Once lubricated, rather with lube or spit, the male would then proceed to stroke in between the close sitting titties. Women, we too could give an up and down motion while the penis is sitting there for an added piece of goodness.

DICK-Cussion: Talk about Titties! Talk about if you like sucking titties or if you like your titties sucked. What did you read that you would like to try? What could your partner practice more of doing? What number are you on the titty chart?

Dick-Cussion

.

Give Me

Some Mo

Now that we have talked about the main body parts, we all should be on the same page. We know about the Noonsie, we know all about the Cock Glock and the different sizes to enjoy, and we are familiar with different shapes and sizes of titties. Up first, we will get a little deeper into how to master the Noonsie. I know I said earlier that the clit is the most important part of the Noonsie, but it isn't the only part that could give off ultimate satisfaction.

Foreplay plays a big part in how the Noonsie reacts as well. The Noonsie is triggered by touch and the brain. Touch is the easiest way out of the two to obtain the right friction you desire. Touch could be done with your hand, tongue, toys, or any other form of contact with the Noonsie. Oral sex is the most popular in my opinion, which all of this is my opinion, to ensure a lubricative setting. Even if the person giving oral sex doesn't quite know what they are doing, oral sex will still add moisture from the mouth for penetration. Another good perk for oral sex during foreplay is awakening the clit. Once the clit is sensitive and the vagina is moisturized, the penetration part becomes much better. During the eating process, you could start opening the Noonsie one finger at a time. A slow twirl of the finger inside while still nibbling on the clit gives a two-part feeling for the female. You can keep it basic with one finger or you can continue to add more fingers depending on the movement of the female. Body language could tell you a lot about if the other person is being pleased or not. So, always pay attention to that.

The other way to stimulate the Noonsie is by making love to the mind. The Noonsie and the mind work together. If the mind is in a good mood and has raging hormonal vibes, then this puts less hassle on waking up the Noonsie. For example, as I mentioned before, watching porn creates a sense in your mind of what a feeling is like from watching other people or from watching yourself! Like my mentor will tell me, "Thinking positive will bring positivity to your life." So, I'm sure that she meant "Thinking about sex will bring good sex into your life" as well. Kissing and rubbing will send signals to the mind and the blood flow increases, enlarging the clitoris. The vagina glands will sweat and the Noonsie becomes wet! See how that works? The mind will get a signal to alert Noonsie that it is time to make it rain.

All the parts work together in most cases. When a penis is involved, it will stroke the walls of the vagina and depending on the size it will also touch the clitoris on the inside and outside. The pleasure is coming from the stroke of the penis along with the breeze action to the clitoris. There is an action I like to call the Jack Rabbit. This is when the guy is stroking in short fast strokes. I laugh about it a lot because, in the younger years, I would hear most females talk about this same action. Maybe because we were younger and the guy had to hurry up and finish before getting caught by the teacher. Believe it or not, this stroke will create an orgasm. What happens is that the Cock Glock is creating a solid pound straight to the G-Spot. The G-spot is like a pinata. If you keep banging and banging it will soon explode. The best position for this is doggy style. Bending over doggy style creates a hallway for the penis to penetrate straight to the front door of the G-Spot. Not saying you cannot reach this spot in other positions but doggy style levels the body for clearer access.

Ladies, while the banging is going on if you want to add some extra sauce to the sex try this trick. If in the doggy style reach your hand back to play with the balls or use your hand to play with yourself. If your partner is one who doesn't mind some balls' action, then he will love the extra attention. Another trick you can do is the infamous throw it back. While he is pounding from the back, throw it back in a water wave motion. Don't be too aggressive because you can throw it back too hard and mess the rhythm up. Messing the rhythm up means nothing though. There will be plenty of strokes where both people are not on the same flow but the job will still get done. Once you become a pro at it, you will be throwing it back, grabbing the balls, and playing with yourself.

The Cock Glock also reacts with the mind. A simple thought could grow the penis in inches right before your eyes. The penis could grow without anyone touching it, as well as shrink back to soft without anyone touching it. A guy told me before that he couldn't get on the hard, and he knew that he wanted to have sex with the female who was right in front of his face. I ask what could have been the problem. He told me that it was because his mind wasn't focused because he was thinking about his side chick instead. True story, but if the two parts aren't on the same mission then sometimes the penis will not get on the hard. Women, please do not think when this happens that you aren't good enough or you are not sexy. Trust me, it happens to the best of us.

Just like the Noonsie, foreplay plays a lot in how the body parts function. You could start off by touching the Cock Glock and rubbing it making sure to touch all parts. The blood flow increases and the Cock Glock wakes up inch by inch. If this doesn't work, the mouth could be the second option. When the penis discovers a warm wet lip on the tip of the head it sends messages that it is about to go down! I'm starting to think that oral sex works so well because the penis is close to the partner's mind when it's in the mouth. Automatic connection!

All of these mini-lessons should help you to figure out what excites your partner and ways to keep the Noonsie moist and the Cock Glock hard without outside tools.

DICK-Cussion: After trying out some of these tips, talk about which tip worked out best for you. Discuss what makes you horny. What helps to get your mind aligned with your body?

Dick-Cussion

Sex Word Play

```
T A G K X C K P L X G L Q O V
I N M M X C C C Q C A Z O K T
L A Z V X B O B I K A J P U M
Z L E T M I L V Q S I N E P B
N Z M J N T G K U L A U X E S
O H C E A A K F T I L A Y B G
O I L M D G C V I B R A T O R
N F I I A U O I U B I Y C R S
S D T B T W C B R W E O U M U
I N O F F I P A O B N A F S S
E F R N G X T B T D U S D Y E
C J I M M W P T O I Q L W S E
K N S B P M C M I G O G I S T
Q E Z Y Q P S E Y E K N J U H
U Q Y J J Q F G R X S E N P I
```

NOONSIE
COCKGLOCK
CLITORIS
SEXUAL
CONDOMS
PUSSY
PENIS
TITTIES
EDUCATION
VIBRATOR
ANAL
BEADS
LUBRICANT

Balls

A Poem by

Nut

Hang low, hang high, some come with a crease.
When you lift them boys up, there's a prize underneath.

Don't go too far Bc you might get hit,
Or end up in some shit.
But just be a little generous and massage a lil bit.

Or you can drip drop drip drap as long as you got some space,
I think they call that tea bagging.
I want mine with a lemon if that's the case.

Roll them around in your hand as if you're about to shoot dice.
I ain't got no balls but I'm sure it feels nice.

But what do I know, this could all just be a rumor.
Just grab two plums and do what y'all did with those
cucumbers.

Fact, the testicles aren't saggy, it's the scrotum that's a lil
looser.
Those boys really hold our future,
Test-ost-er-rone yeaa that's what it is.
But if your dude showing out, then fuck them kids.

Condoms & Lube

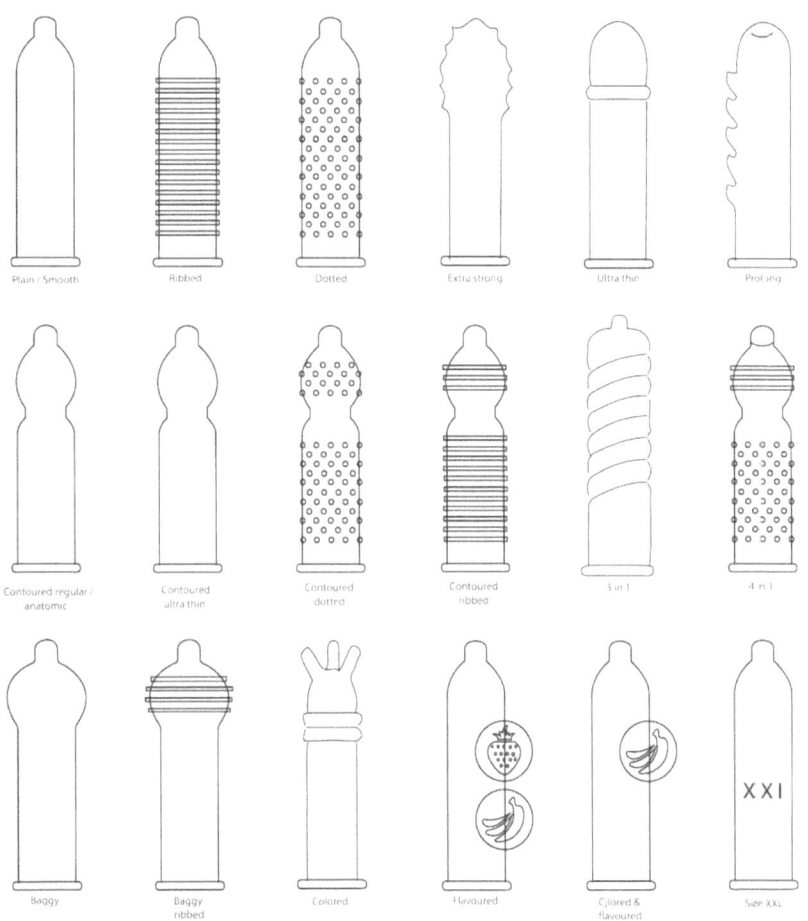

Plain / Smooth	Ribbed	Dotted	Extra strong	Ultra thin	Prolong
Contoured regular / anatomic	Contoured ultra thin	Contoured dotted	Contoured ribbed	3 in 1	4 in 1
Baggy	Baggy ribbed	Colored	Flavoured	Colored & flavoured	Size XXL

What You Got On Boy?

Car Sex

A Story by Janae

Car sex could be hell and heaven at the same time. I remember when I was 19 years old and was home from college on our Christmas break. This was one of the worst times to try and have a freaky link because I was living on campus, and back at home there were no low key places to have sex. While in high school, we had our parent's home while they were away at work or we just stayed at a friend's house, whose parents didn't care if we ran a hoe house. Where could I go this time? I didn't know if we would have sex or not but I still needed a location suitable for all the vibes.

Terry wasn't from my hometown. I met him on Myspace and he was traveling through to go see his family. Well, at least that's what he told me. We had been talking via messenger for about two weeks now. Once I told him I would be coming home, he wanted to link just so we can meet in person. I couldn't think of a secure spot to meet so I told him let's meet up at the school in the parking lot. No one was there being that school was out for the holidays and traffic was never heavy in the area. He pulled up in a two-door Honda Civic. I made the decision to invite him over into my mom's Dodge Ram, which I had been driving since I was home.

Just like I imagined, it didn't take us more than 7 minutes to be kissing in the backseat with his hand around my neck. I could tell from the way he licked my neck that he was kind of a rough guy when it came to sex. We never talked about it online but the way the girls were all over his page, I figured he wouldn't be an armature either. He took his shirt off and threw it to the side. A little skinnier than I thought, but it was okay. Terry kissed my neck again and tugged on my shirt for me to raise my arms so he could pull it over my head. This guy was fast with all of his actions but he wasn't giving me enough time to enjoy his kisses. No words were being said, just fast movement and quick kisses. He had me all the way down to my underwear. Maybe I wasn't used to having sex in the car, but why did we have to get all the way to undress for car sex? I laid back and he took off his pants. This was going faster than I expected. He climbed on top of me but I closed my legs to ensure that he was going to put on a condom first. Terry was cool but he had a chest flatter than a credit card and I was not about to let him hit it raw. He gave me one of those rough kisses again, so as to give himself more time to reach in his pockets to get the condom. The car was so dark that it was hard for him to see but finally I heard the wrapper being torn and the rubber-like smell filled the area. In order to get back on the hard, he played with my coochie for about two seconds. Yep! That was rough too. I don't know what he could have been so mad about, but he was not as smooth as I pictured. Although he was rough while rubbing his fingers across my coochie, I was wet as a faucet. Hovering over me to get in a comfortable position made it easy for me to slide up and rest my head on the arm of the door. There it was. He stuck it in and started doing push-ups inside of me. I had my hands wrapped around his tiny waist while he moved up and down, up and down. It felt okay but I was too busy thinking about the crook I was going to have in my neck in the morning because of the angle my body was being twisted into. Hopefully, it felt good to one of us. He changed up the stroke and started charging hard inside of my vagina walls. Between him being so rough and my neck hanging on the edge of the handle made this experience not worth pulling in front of my alma mater taking up parking spaces. One of us needed a lesson. I stopped him so I could scoot up and rest my head better. This position was giving me hell. I pushed him off of me and told him to sit down. Maybe if I had a little more control it would go a lot smoother. We changed positions and I started riding him in the middle of the seat. I wanted to ride him slow so he could get an idea of what kind of sex I was used to. Slow was how I started. Really couldn't tell if it felt good to him because he wasn't that much of a moaner. Even when he was on top of me he didn't moan too often. Trust me, I wasn't a cowgirl but this wasn't my first rodeo. Trying to be sexy, I started twirling around on top of him. I had never tried this motion before but something told me he was enjoying it. He finally moaned. I was proud of myself but went too far when I tried my twirl motion while bouncing to the tip of his penis. It slipped out and I grabbed his penis to place it right back in but just my luck! The condom was gone.

I sat my bare ass next to him to avoid bending over in his face. We both looked around on the floor and I could only find the condom wrapper. My second thought was maybe it was inside of me. I laid down, back on that hard ass armrest, while he played Mr. Grey's Anatomy and placed his finger inside of my vagina. Yet again, this guy was rough with the fingers, maneuvering all-around in my coochie. Nothing! We turned the lights on just to get a better look. He searched under the seat, and while doing so he started pulling up his pants. I took a quick glance at him and realized that he wasn't all of that in person at all. Myspace does know how to fool you. He said that he's sure it's around, under the chair, someplace but we shouldn't risk staying in the parking lot with the light on at this time of night. That made sense but regardless if I agreed or not, he was already dressed. He hugged me and said he would call me once he arrived at his destination and to just check under the front seat. Okay, roughneck!

On my way back home, I questioned if I really saw him put on a condom or not. I know I smelled the condom in the beginning but I was so wet on the stick in, I didn't notice it. All I could think about was how bamboozled I felt. A MySpace dude had tricked me into thinking we used a condom.

A week later, I was back in my dorm having a discussion with one of my male classmates, Jon, about our time at home for the holidays. We've had sex before but it was something I could do without for the rest of my life. We laughed hysterically until he asked if he could eat me out. As I mentioned, I could do without his sex, so I turned it down. The next question was if he could feel it for a little while. Fingering was no longer a big deal back then, so I didn't see an issue with that. He reached in my pants and started feeling inside of me. It was wayyy smoother than what I received the week prior and I was wet as hell again. Maybe I should get some quick sex since I was wet and ready. He slowed down before I could really feel it. He stared in my eyes and did one last finger twirl before bringing his finger out of my coochie. He took his hand out of my pants and behold!! There it was. The long lost condom and a ridiculous smell right in my face. It was safe to say I took two losses. Jon was never going to eat me out and Terry never made it to his destination because I never heard from him again.

ondoms! Condoms!! Condoms!!! That is all they preached growing up. The adults could smell the sex in the air and wanted to make sure we all were protected. They didn't tell us how dry and irritated condoms would be. We didn't care at that moment though, we just knew we could get a free bag of lifestyle condoms from the clinic or from the sex education class that we skipped when we had plans to go have sex. Everybody had at least one or two condoms on them that were too old to use but we ended up using them anyway or giving them to someone else. If you still use these condoms, please, please, please grow up! We are going to talk about some better condom options for couples who are just starting.

Condoms come with so many different options. Take a look at the chart. Making sex fun could start with the condom option if you are into using them. Condoms come ribbed, dotted, thin, colored, hell it's some with three heads on the top. If you ever wanted more than one meat inside you at a time, the three-headed condom will come close to giving you that experience. For those who like to experiment with different flavors, there are condoms for you too. You can choose from strawberry flavored, blueberry flavored, vanilla flavored, and mint-flavored to name a few. I would say, don't knock them until you try them. Even if you don't believe in using condoms during oral sex, you should at least try a flavored one. The flavor is on the outside of the condom. Giving two sucks on a flavored condom and then taking the condom off but still sucking will leave the taste in your mouth for a few more sucks.

Magnums are very popular condoms. Magnums are made for the larger size Cock Glocks, thereby giving it a better fit and not as tight as regular condoms. Ladies be careful though. I know of some men out here carrying around Magnum condoms but there is nothing magnum about the dick size. Wearing an oversize condom has its consequences, especially if the condom is already too big and the Noonsie extra wet. The condom will sure slip right off and inside of the Noonsie. Now, we are stuck with a condom inside and a soft dick. No fun at all!

Lube and condoms go well together. One of the main reasons people don't like wearing condoms is because it just doesn't feel like the real thing. It gives a dryer feeling to the strokes. Some new condoms were created that mimic the real feeling of bare sex. I can't lie, the condom game stepped up a lot from when I was younger. There is a much better selection to choose from, but when all else fails, use lube. Lube is the magic icing to sex. Even with a condom, when using lube, you will feel more moisture and sometimes won't even notice that a condom is there. The trickiest thing about lube is making sure to select the best kind for both of you. Some females could be really sensitive and could have an allergic reaction to the lube and condom. Before trying out anything new, especially something that will touch the skin, test it out. Take the lube and place a small portion on your skin for five minutes, and if nothing happens within those five minutes you may be okay. Also, when selecting lube, you want to be careful with the type of lube. Oil-based lubes could dysfunction the condom or rip it due to the consistency of the oil. Water-based lubes are better for the condom and the

Noonsie. The chances of getting an infection from a water-based lube are lower because the lube base is composed of water products and hopefully, we use water on the regular.

Using lube without a condom is magical also. Please don't be embarrassed about using lube. Rather, if you are a female and would like a smoother less friction sex lifestyle, or if you are a male and want your partner to be wetter longer, using lube would help. This doesn't mean that you are dry for a female. Some lubes are created to give a different experience while having sex. Some lubes give off a heated sensation and/or cooling sensation while at the same time adding more moisture. In most cases, it makes sex easier. You don't have to start sex off by using lube. Lube could be added after rounds or during a position change with easy fast applying instructions.

DICK-Cussion: Talk about condoms that you've used before and some that you would like to try. Discuss the different types of lube and flavors you will also try and on which body parts.

Dick-Cussion

_____
_____
_____
_____
_____
_____
_____
_____
_____
_____
_____
_____
_____
_____
_____
_____
_____
_____
_____
_____
_____
_____
_____
_____
_____
_____
_____
_____
_____
_____
_____

It's Nut-O'clock

I Said What I Said

A Poem by Nut

Long sex, I hate it.
My moans, I start to fake it.

My legs aren't shaking bc I just can't take it.
Not once do I want you to think that I'm basic.

But please sit down, let me give you the tea.
I only have about 3 more ughhhhs left in me.

I know Missy said we don't want no minute man,
But long sex I just can't stand.

Maybe I should keep my mouth shut.

Is this menopause, or should I give men a pause,
Because y'all men do pause when y'all trying not to nut.

Adrian Pnut Steward

It started off great don't get me wrong,
But you've been going longer than a gospel song.

You've done killed the box,
I can't Eee eww that's dead.

I HATE LONG SEX.
I said what I said!

There is no real set time to how long sex should be. It can range from seconds to minutes, to hours all depending on different circumstances and your opinion of when sex starts. I've heard couples say that foreplay is considered the start of sex. This timing could be different for couples that believe sex doesn't start until actual intercourse. I am one person who believes that sex doesn't start until the Cock Glock has entered the chat room. At this point, we are on a mission to make it to the finish line. Whatever takes place between the start and the finish line all are a part of the race. How fast do you want to get there?

The length of sex does not determine if the sex was good. Trust, long sex does not always mean better sex. When a guy nuts fast, research (my friends) says this means the Noonsie was A1. That could be true, but there are other reasons why males nut quickly. The good thing is, if nutting fast is an issue for you, there are several methods to try and improve the amount of time you could last. The first option is masturbating before you have sex. In most cases, the first nut comes quicker than the second if you are going for more than one round. Masturbating gets the first nut out the way. This gives males some time to recharge. Receiving head is also another method to get the first nut out the way. By the time, you're up and ready for sexual intercourse, the next nut will have time to make itself to the front.

The next option will be the "slow, stop, change position." This option happens during the process of having sex. When the male feels a nut coming he should begin to slow down his strokes, come to a stop and then change positions. When he has stopped and in the process of changing positions, the nut slows down from coming out. I think of it as the nut taking a break from running to the finish line. The pauses during strokes only add on a couple more seconds before a nut. A major position change is a oral sex. Once the male has stopped stroking, begin to give the female head to add on some more time. Not only does this help the nut from coming so quick, but this position change adds on moisture. The nut will be delayed and the Noonsie will be wet for more play. The slow down, stop, change position, is tough to control if the girl is on top. The feeling will be so good you could barely tell her to slow down, stop, change position. Be careful which position you are in if you try this method.

The most efficient method is the blue pill. I refer to it as the "gas station blue pill." Mostly, all gas stations sell this pill right in front of the register at check out. You can't miss it because it's a blue sex pill. Taking one of these pills before sexual intercourse will have your Cock Glock fully charged and ready to go! It increases your stamina and improves your erections. Guys have said, they could really tell the difference between taking the pill and not taking the pill before sex. Even after the first nut, when taking this pill, chances are high that the Cock Glock will be ready for more action.

Also, remember that your mind has some control over how long it takes to nut as well. While in the act of having sex, try not to think so hard about what is taking place. Once you learn how to control yourself, it will be much easier to maintain stamina, unless the Noonsie is really A1.

The length it takes for a male to nut, matters to females also. The timing will have to be long enough for the female to release or have an orgasm. Females, if you have sex with a minute man, there are ways to help you climax before the sex ends. Just like the male, masturbating prior to sex helps. When the female masturbates before sex it enlarges the clitoris. In a previous chapter, I mentioned how the clitoris is a big deal. Well, I actually mention this throughout the book, but once the clitoris has grown, it makes it easier for the female to climax over and over. After the first nut, the clit remains sensitive. If the clit is already sensitive during sexual intercourse, the climax would not take as long and the Noonsie will be prepared for penetration. Instead of masturbating, the female could receive oral sex and awake the clitoris that way. Making it wet and ready for another orgasm.

Stimulation to clit during sex will help the female to reach orgasm faster. Depending on the position, while penetration is taking place, caress the clit. It doesn't matter who plays with the clit, just make it happen. If the couple is in missionary style, the woman should massage her clit during the stroking motion. The Noonsie will be stroked and the clit will be entertained.

Sex toys, which I will go more into detail in the next chapter, are great tools to use. For example, the male could wear a vibrating cock ring during sex. The cock ring will send vibrations to the clit. This could be used in any position. This is similar to massaging the clit on your own, but having a toy to do it for you. The vibration sensation will make the clit more sensitive during sexual intercourse without the man having to stroke in uncomfortable positions or with a hand in the way. If the man gets excited about the female massaging herself during sex, then that equals a double win.

A minuteman could do all the tricks in the world to stop himself from nutting too fast, but if the noonsie is A1, then the noonsie is just A1. In other cases, the sex could have been going on for a while, and the nut is still nowhere to be found. If you really only had time for a quickie and the time is taking way too long, try incorporating other things. Oral sex, playing with the balls, freaky sex talk and so many other small things could get the nut out if the man's mind is focused on busting a nut. How long sex should be is solely dependent on the couple. Some like to take their time and enjoy the moment while others like to get to the finish line and move along to doing something else. Even if the sex didn't last long, it could have still gotten the job done for both people.

DICK-Cussion: Go over with your partner if you prefer sex to last a long time or quickies will do. Discuss the different options you would like to try. What could the other person do to ensure satisfaction before the time is up?

Dick-Cussion

_____
_____
_____
_____
_____
_____
_____
_____
_____
_____
_____
_____
_____
_____
_____
_____
_____
_____
_____
_____
_____
_____
_____
_____
_____
_____
_____
_____
_____
_____
_____
_____

Let's Play

72 Inch

A Story by

Luke

Tonight, I wanted to do something different. She was already freakier than me, so I had to think outside the box. When we first met, I could tell she was way more experienced than I was just from the sex pictures that hung on her living room wall. LIVING ROOM WALL! The first thing you see on the wall is a female getting her pussy ate out and on the opposite wall a man sitting down with his dick hanging off his leg. I don't know if I should be upset because buddy's dick was bigger than mine, or should I be turned on from the fact she was open about sex! The first time we had sex I nutted faster than Chic-Fila service. We went two rounds and I still wasn't able to hold my nut in to make sure she busted one. After I nut the second time in like twenty-two seconds, she just smiled and rubbed my back. This made me feel like I was a son of hers who just lost the championship game in pee wee football.

This time was going to be different though. I had been jacking my dick for three days straight so that he or I wouldn't get too excited after seeing her fat thick ass bend over showing that pussy print from the front. Damn! Dick getting hard just thinking about it. What made matters worse was that she didn't moan like I was killing her shit. I was pounding in that pussy with all my strength and she barely said a word. Don't get me wrong, I've killed some pussies before so I know what I'm doing but this girl was different.

Of course, she knew I was going to try and hit the next time we linked up, but she had no idea the tricks I had up my sleeve. I didn't want to feel intimidated by that big dick bastard posted up on her wall, so I invited her to my crib. It was player like. I had a couple of good pieces I can brag about, like my Hennesey wall full of empty Hennessy bottles or my signed Players Club poster on the wall behind my 72inch TV. My TV has seen plenty of naked females and a majority of them love taking a look at themselves after I've put it down.

She was into that kinky shit. I watched 50 Shades of Grey for a quick second just to get some ideas of what freaky shit I should do. Just like I thought, nothing caught my eye to experiment with. Her ass was too big to have it in a sling going back and forth off my door. I did live in some apartments, so I couldn't afford to break anything. I went with my next plan. I started watching porn the night before to see what moves those big black ass niggas were doing! Yet again, I ended up jacking off and falling asleep before I could finish the video. Didn't learn shit! I only had about two hours to figure out what the hell I could do to impress this chick without looking like a fool.

Food and sex goes great together. I remember this one female that slurped some grape syrup off my dick. It felt good as hell until it was time for me to stick it in and my penis wouldn't slide in and out. The syrup became sticky and I had to wash it off in the sink. By the time I finished getting all the syrup off, shawty said she was tired and wanted to cuddle. I ain't even with that cuddling shit but shawty was bad. Maybe I could use something else like jelly. Naw, my sister told me not to be placing all types of stuff inside females because that's how they get bacteria vaginas or whatever they call it. I just knew my ex used to have vagina cream all over the bathroom floor.

The last thing I could come up with was taking a ride to the sex store and getting some of that good lube. I've used it before but never bought any. My homie used to steal some from Walmart but we are grown now. Who knows, I might find another freak inside waiting for a young bull like myself.

I got to the store and asked the lady at the register if they had lube. She looked at me like I was crazy. Hell, yea, they had lube! She walked me to a wall full of lube. They had flavored lube, small pouches, large pouches, lube that looked like snot, warming lube, mannn like I tell you, all kinds of lube. I didn't know which one to choose. I needed something that said I was used to being freaky but also something that made me look like I was being romantic. The worker was standing right over my shoulder like I was going to steal her shit or something, so I asked her which lube she used before. She pointed out a purple box and told me this one will have the female wet for hours even after the sex was over. I didn't need that one. I ain't want her still wet to go give another clown some pussy.

The worker asked me what kind I was looking for. I explained to her that I hadn't any type of lube in mind but something to add a lil razzle-dazzle to the sex. She started walking to another section of the store. It was dark over here. Yeaaaa, this was where the freak section was. She showed me a wall of kinky sex toys. Vibrators the size of my arm, handcuffs, some weird-ass ankle bracelets, and balls you place inside the female's mouth just to name a few. One stood out to me! It was a small penis like vibrator. If I pulled this out and played with it in her pussy right before I stuck King Kong in, I would for sure turn her on and would be the freak of the night. When I got to the cash register the lady just smiled at me. She knew what time it was! She asked if I needed any lube tonight. Nope! This small toy didn't need any extra wetness. It was just a tad bit bigger than my thumb. She rang me up and told me to have fun. It was time for me to put it down.

I got back to the crib and waited for her to come over. I had about three shots of, you know it, Hennesey! I was ready to show her the new toy I bought and get busy. The doorbell rang and already my dick started jumping. Calm down man, we are about to dive into some sweet pussy in just a second. I opened the door and there she was, standing there with one of those lace wigs on down to her butt and some leather tights with a low cut ballerina shirt on. She had on red lipstick. I don't know why but red was now my favorite color. I greeted her with a hug and this dumb ass look on my face. She switched her ass to sit on my leather couch right where all of the fine ladies sat. I offered her a drink to start the night off right. After about ten minutes of talking I was ready to get to work.

I moved a little closer to her on the chair and sniffed her neck, she laughed. I took my tongue and licked her all the way down to her collar bone. "Let me eat it," I said. The first time we had sex I was too excited to eat it. Either that or I came too quick and was too embarrassed to stick my dry ass tongue down low. This time though, I was going to show her this whirlwind. I started eating the fuck out of her pussy. Her pretty pussy lips overlapped my lips and I started vibrating my tongue. I took my pointing finger and poked in her hole real slow. While my index finger was going in and out slowly, I took my thumb and rubbed her clit at the same time. I could tell I was already being freaky enough for her because she was moaning this time. You mean to tell me all I needed to do was bring out the magic fingers.

After about ten seconds of more slow finger fucking, I told her to hold on while I grabbed something else. This small penis toy I bought to stick in her was going to blow her mind! My 72inch TV was about to be front and center of the best sex ever. When I got back to the chair she was fingering herself and staring at me with her mouth wide open. The red lipstick was still shining bright and your boy was ready to drop something in it. I couldn't go straight to doing that because I wanted to show off the new toy. She reached out for the toy and started licking on the fake balls. Damn, that was sexy to me and made me realize I indeed picked out the right toy. She whispered in between licks, "I didn't know you were into toys." Well, I wasn't, but tonight I was trying to impress her ass. She pulled me closer and told me to take off my shorts. I dropped my shorts to the floor. My dick was standing at attention. She started sucking the tip of the head and went back to the toy licking the balls. She went back and forth for about five minutes. I was starting to become jealous of that small dick piece of toy I bought. The head was feeling too good for her that she could not stop licking the balls of some plastic ass piece.

After the last lick on Mr. Small Dick, she asked if I was ready. I said hell, yea! She stood in front of me and grabbed my dick. I knew after two strokes that I was going to cum this time and didn't even feel bad about it. She was like, are we using the toy? I was really done with that lil bastard but remember, I said I wanted to be freaky and show her a good time. I nodded yes real slow, reaching for the toy so that I can let her finally feel it. She said, "Naw, let me do you first." What the fuck!! After cursing her out and making her to get out of my spot was when I noticed that My dumb ass had brought an anal toy and that freak thought she was going to use it on me. I guess I'm not as freaky as I wished to be. I'm just going to settle for a basic female to drink this Hennessy in front of my 72inch TV.

Play with Me

My favorite part about sex is being able to be creative. Sex is not just a lay down and you lay down type of party, well unless you are just that basic when it comes to the bedroom or the coffee shop. Playing with different types of condoms, lubes, and sex toys are great for spicing things up a bit. There are so many different choices and combinations to play with so as to ensure that the same boring sex doesn't take place. It should be no reason not to have a fun-filled, exciting sex life.

When I was growing up, I would go inside my mom's dresser drawer to find some socks. One day, I looked into the wrong dresser drawer by mistake. I was a little confused as to why she had a small back massager and some underwear with a hole in the front. The massager was so small that it could fit in your ear. Well, that's what I thought. That was my first time seeing a sex toy and clearly didn't know what it was for. Twenty-five years later, I could say that I know how to use just about all of them.

The picture shows a number of sex toys and all of them could be used in different ways. Sex toys are whips, vibrators, butt plugs, anal beads, handcuffs, blindfolds, sex dolls, penis pumpers, just to name a few. When picking out sex toys, there are a number of different options to choose from. Let's take a vibrator for example. A vibrator could come in so many shapes and sizes. Depending on the purpose you will have different groups to select from. Rather you want a big one, a small one, one made for two people or one that could be used during anal, it's a group with each type. Small vibrators, also sometimes referred to as bullets, are for clit stimulation purposes. Bullets could be placed right on the clit while the vibrator taps until an orgasm is conceived. There are some bullets that come with two small vibrators attached. For these, you could use it with a partner at the same time, or it could be used on the female at the same time. One is inserted inside the hole and one stimulates the clit.

There are bigger vibrators the size of real Cock Glocks. They also come in different colors so that buyers could have a choice as to which race they wanted to make love with. These are usually inserted inside the hole of choice for penetration. Anal beads are another type of sex items to discuss. Everyone might not be open to trying anal beads. They are beads you put inside of your butt and pull out. Like I mentioned before, the G-spot is a little bit closer to the back allowing anal beads to slide and rub across it during a pull-out. Women and men use anal beads. You could pull them out yourself or have your partner pull them out for you.

Cock Rings are vibrating rings that fit around the Cock Glock. The vibrations from the cock ring are felt all the way around the balls. During penetration, the vibration from the penis will send a vibration to the Noonsie. While using the cock ring, a good position is missionary style. Penetrate as you would regularly do but take long slow strokes so that the Noonsie will feel the Cock Glock along with the vibration from the cock ring around the clit area. Cock rings are made to fit snuggled around the penis making the blood flow increase around the head of the penis. When it is time to release, the nut will be stronger due to the blood flow. Although cock rings are easy to use, it may be uncomfortable to some men until they are used to having something tight and vibrating around the Cock Glock during sex or oral sex.

Fifty Shades of Gray showed us what we could do with ropes and sex swings. This is for the spicey couples who really want to take things to the next level. Being tied up during sex could definitely be a turn on. You are submissive to your partner and they have full control. At this point, you will have to be prepared for the most. Door saddles and sex swings help a lot with tougher positions. They are made to help with balance and improves posture during certain positions. Like ropes and handcuffs, sex swings and saddles illuminates the control you have since you are buckled down.

On the go, toys are my favorite. Some vibrators and cock rings are small enough to fit inside of your pocket. Smaller vibrators are made to be discreet. This means that you can pull it out and play at any time, any place. Just imagine you and your partner stuck in the car for a while or just sitting in traffic, sounds like a great time to pull out some toys and have a good time. Technology has upgraded the sex game in a major way. Companies created toys that are Bluetooth and can be controlled by remote control or a cell phone. For example, a vibrator is placed inside the Noonsie like a tampon. The couple goes out for the night allowing the man to control the vibrator. The woman could enjoy quick vibrations while sitting at the dinner table. This is a sure way to help prepare for dessert later at the house.

I had a conversation with one of my homeboys about using toys in the bedroom. He was against it and said that his lady shouldn't have to use a toy when she has him. I suggested that he tried it with her to ease the jealousy of a battery-operated device. Playing with toys may be new for some people. Just like my homeboy, he didn't see a point for a woman in a relationship to use a vibrator. Did she believe his sex wasn't good enough? Who knows. Both partners should want to use sex toys to make it worth it. Start off with something easy to use and then make your way to the big guns.

DICK-cussion: Talk to your partner about using toys. Would you use them? Do you mind if your partner uses them? Should they use them without you? How far are you willing to go with using sex toys?

Dick-Cussion

Assume the Position

Sex Education Part III

A Poem by

Nut

Sex education part three.
The pleasure is not for you but for me.
So, let's get into the V!
Or some people may call it, the P.U.S.S.Y

Why the hell y'all change it up, when y'all hear us moan?
One wrong tongue stroke could get us out our cumming zone,
Not Comfort zone because don't shit be comfortable.

You be laying on my leg,
now it's going dead,
gotta cramp on my side,
Now the feeling just died.

Like Damn!

It's only one zone that you need to focus on.

If you make the right move that could really take us home.

All that hoking and poking, yea that ain't it.
Just focus on the center and caress the clit.

It has about 8000 nerves I can't make this up.
Some of y'all still can't find one but be ready to fuck.

Now let's talk,
Because not all of us have that WAP,
But that ain't always our fault.

If you're looking for the WAPs,
Try to figure out how many licks it takes to get to the center of
it pleaseee.

Now, if you're looking for that waterfall, you gotta help us get
like that.
Like the Great Khia once said, my neck, my back...

Lick my pussy and my crack

"Pose"

T hink of all the positions you do while having sex. I bet some of y'all could only think of three, the front, from the back, and from the side. Although all of those positions are major positions, there are plenty more positions to try out. When the sex is getting too good, we tend to let our body do whatever. You could end up on your neck with one of your legs behind your arm and your ear on the floor but with good sex, you wouldn't even care! So far in this book, we know what good sex is so it's time to dive into some positions. Literally!

The first position you probably tried was missionary aka on top. Why? That's the position you see in most sex scenes, those PG sex scenes especially. The man looks at the lady with those googly eyes and then takes off his shirt right before climbing on top of her. It happens in all PG-13 love movies. You see, I said PG-13! Meaning let's step it up to a little more Rated R positions. Don't get me wrong, PG-13 positions paved the way for Rated R positions to take place.

The first position on the chart shows the female riding the male with her back towards him. I like to call this position the CowGirl. The woman is bouncing that ass on the Cock Glock and her hair in the wind like she is straddling a horse. For support and balance, women, don't be afraid to hold onto the man's thighs. That's why they are there. Even if you do this position while sitting down on a chair or the edge of the bed, you still can hold onto the thighs for a better bounce. Men, if you can handle it, grab her by the waist and help move her in the motions that work for you. This doesn't mean that you should take her out of her groove but it's a team thing.

Riding the opposite way, you could use the same technique. To help the lady balance better, the guy should bend his knees as if they were the back of a chair (shown in picture). This posture uplifts the buns, thereby giving her an angle to ride on versus flat land. Every time she bounces, the Noonsie drops first and then the ass follows. Ladies, while riding it, find a groove that works for you. Stay in that motion and pay attention to the moans. If he moans during certain movements, it simply means he enjoys that rhythm. If you are not able to find a bounce that is comfortable for you, place a pillow underneath the man's butt. This elevates his penis and it is easier to bounce up and down by adding more height.

When the man is on top they tend to adjust your legs to their liking. The lady could do a full split with her legs open in the air or have the legs closed as if she was a baby and the man was about to change her diaper. Play with the legs during this position. The man is in more control because this is his stroking zone. To get deeper in the Noonsie, the man should lift his partner's butt up and drop the Cock Glock in from an angle. I can't teach you the stroke game. It is something that you will have to learn while doing it. You should be able to feel the shape of the vagina and find a steady stroke that will make the woman feel good and you.

Hitting it from the back or what most of us call doggy style is another position with layers. First, this position is a teamwork position. Although the man is the one standing up, while his partner is free to "throw it bike!" For example, the male is stroking while the woman is bent over. With each stroke or some of the strokes, the woman will bounce her ass back. After a while of the man stroking and the woman throwing it back, the two will become in sync and the position will be as easy as clapping your hands. Remember what I told you earlier, you have to learn your partner very well. Some women do not like throwing it back and some men prefer for the woman not to throw it back if the woman does not decide to throw it back she will need to just make sure her back arch is legit. The way the back is arched is very important in this position. The way the woman has her arch and ass tooted up will determine how the penis will be dropped inside.

After a while in this position, you may find yourself laying flat on top of each other. This means that the sex is good. Neither one of you could hold your weight and decide to do the lazy dog. This is okay! The arch is still important in this case although the woman is not on all fours anymore. During this position, while maintaining the arch, the woman should take this time to play with her clit. There is never a wrong time for the lady to show love to herself. Rub the clit for a more sensational feeling while the man covers the back for you.

The Seesaw is a position that merges doggy style and riding. The male should lay on his back with his legs open and knees bent. The woman should get on all fours just like she would in doggy style but placing her legs underneath the male's bent legs, connecting the Noonsie to the Cock Glock. Since the woman is not on top like regular riding, she would move back and forth like a seesaw. Warning, the Cock Glock must be big enough to perform this position. This position is also good if the woman knows how to back that thing up as The Great Juvenile informed us to do early on.

The side angle is a top tier position. I've heard the side is the best position for morning sex. You just wake up roll on your side and get to work. There is a slight throw bike in this position. The woman's leg could stay straight right beside the man, or she could wrap her leg around the man's leg for a closer penetration. Laying on the side is no different from the other positions. You could lay on the side and still form a doggy style position.

In order to achieve a more complicated position, you would have to work on your flexibility. That goes for the male and female. If you know that you are about to engage in some all-night position changing mind-blowing sex, stretch! Trust me, stretching is key to a lot of movement. Stretching together makes it even wilder because, by the time you are two minutes into stretching, somebody is ready to have sex.

All of the oral sex positions shown are all correct. There is no wrong way to engage in oral sex. The most teamwork oral position is the 69. This is when the woman and man partake in oral sex at the same time. This could be done laying down or if you have balance and strength, standing up. Honestly, I don't think this position is a fair position. Someone always gets the better bargain. This position is fun and gets both body parts wet and ready for the main event.

All in all, there is no wrong position. Whatever works for you and your partner is the best way to go. Even this includes creating your own positions. Just be sure to write to me so that I can add it to Volume II!

DICK-Cussion: Go over the position picture and talk about each one and how you feel about it. What positions have you tried and which ones do you want to try? Do you prefer the "throw bike" method?

Dick-Cussion

Re-DICK-ulous

Trip

A Story by

Carlos

ow 29-Seat A and B. It was Valentine's Day weekend, so what better time to take a quick trip out of town. My girl, Reign, was slowly walking in front of me to find our row. The plane was packed as I imagined. I could see a lot of couples had the same idea to get away for the weekend. Since we waited last minute, the only flight left was 10:00 pm. Lucky us, the passenger on the end had to be reseated since her seatbelt didn't work. The flight was going to be three hours long, just enough time for me to take a quick nap. Reign sat on the inside because she loved the window view at night. I made myself comfortable and it was time for take-off.

As soon as the lights went off, Reign placed her head on my shoulder to get ready for her nap. I wrapped my arm around her to make her more relaxed. I knew that she really wanted to get a nap but I held her breast in my hand just to see if she would let me carry on. She gave me that, "boy stop" look instead. It was okay though because I knew as soon as we walked into that hotel room it was going down. I can't lie, my dick was on hard just from that quick tease. I grabbed her breast again to try my luck for a second time. It worked! She didn't give me a funny look this time. She continued to rest her head on my shoulder while I thumb wrestled with her nipple. Dick was really on hard now. I didn't let myself get too excited because she wasn't really with that public affair stuff. I was just happy to be flying in the air with a nice nipple at my fingertips.

I played with her boob until I heard her baby snores on my shoulder. I've always heard a good massage will do the trick. Now that she was asleep, I pulled out my phone with my other arm and started scrolling Twitter. It was late, so all down my timeline were the freaks that came out at night. People were talking about how single they were, how spoiled they were, and of course how horny they were. I fell in the horny category but I only had about two more hours until I was in another state and had my sweetmeat in some fresh flewed out coochie.

I kept scrolling. The next post was a girl giving head on the hood of the car in broad daylight. My dick instantly got hard. It was only a 24-second clip. It wasn't long enough to see the outcome but it was long enough for my manhood to start poking. I grabbed Reign's breast again to see if she would like to play this time. She woke up and just changed positions. She turned her body all the way over to face the window but still had her head on my shoulder. I guess that meant no more holding the nipple.

I had on some sweatpants. I rubbed my penis to calm it down. After rubbing it about four times, I thought why not go ahead and do my thing to help me sleep real quick. I rubbed my dick from the outside of my pants for about two more minutes. Yea, I might as well just handle business. I placed my hands in my pants and started jacking real slow. My girl knew I masturbated sometimes when she didn't want to give it up but I still didn't want her to wake up to me pulling on my dick on the airplane. The more I jacked the faster I got. I was missing some moisture though. My dick was extra dry because I had just taken a hot shower prior to going to the airport. I didn't see the point of jacking a dry dick on the plane so I stopped. I could just wait until I got to the hotel as I said.

I rested my head on my girl's head so I could go to sleep and make time move faster. I dozed off. Suddenly, a hand touched my dick gently. Finally, my girl was with the freaky stuff, or was I dreaming? I kept my eyes closed either way because I didn't want the rubbing to stop. Yep, I did just what females do when their dude is trying to hit in the morning while they still fake sleep but somehow know how to toot it up for the dick to fit right in. We know y'all don't be asleep but we like to play along. Anyway, all she had to do was go inside my pants to get me all the way right. Instead of going inside of my sweatpants, a hand took my hand and placed it on some wet coochie. I instantly woke up. It wasn't my girl; it was the girl who had to switch seats. I had to be dreaming. I looked over to see if my girl was awake but she was still out like a light. The girl next to me just smiled and rubbed her coochie with my hand underneath her dress. The bad thing was, she was wet as hell and I didn't want her to stop. At this point, my dick was throbbing. I knew this wasn't right, so I pulled my hand from under her dress. I should have known from that Cititrends pocketbook that this girl was a freak.

I shook my head at her to let her know I was not about to risk waking my girl up. Instead of this freak moving back to her seat, she started playing with herself right in front of me. I looked around to see what everyone else was doing because I knew somebody had to be watching. The plane was quiet and everyone was asleep. I took a hard swallow because she knew and I knew, I wanted to partake in digging that coochie. She pulled her hand out from under her dress and placed one of the fingers in her mouth. The way she sucked on her finger, my dick wouldn't stand a chance. Her face showed that she enjoyed her sweet-savory flavor. I guess she could tell from the glow in my eyes that I was into everything she was doing. She placed the other finger on my lip and before I knew it, I had a mouth full. She then took her other hand and started playing in her coochie. I had to make it stop or wake up!

My girl was still asleep. Her head was still on my shoulder and she did not have a clue about the freak shit that was taking place in the seat next to me.

It was time for me to really end this and send shawty back to her seat. I pushed her leg so she could get up and go. I nudged her a little too hard because my girl moved her head to change positions. I was about to really be in some deep shit. Shawty needs to hurry and take her and her tight, wet, taste like Fiji water ass pussy back to her seat. My girl wrapped my arm back around her still asleep but this time placed my hand on her breast again. What was going on!? I didn't start rubbing on her breast until it really registered that she wanted to play that sleep trick. Shawty on my right still fingering herself and now my girl on my left wants me to play with her. I gave shawty the look to leave. She gave me the sad puppy face back. If she did not get up before my girl noticed, it was about to be murder in the air.

My girl still had her eyes closed while she moved her right leg on top of mine. She really wanted to play the sleep game. The truth was, she wanted me to reach in her jogging pants and finger her until she came. I had to take action quickly before she opened her eyes, wondering why the hell I wasn't twirling in her coochie. Shawty on the right watched me finger my girl and moaned in my ear while the breathing sounds my girl made slowly came out. This was the worst, freakiest shit I had ever been in. Not to mention how wet my girl was and how loud she was becoming. She started moaning as if no one else was on the plane. Shawty made matters worse and started rubbing on my girl's breast at the same time! I wanted someone to wake me up if I was dreaming for real this time. The good thing was, she was still playing sleep. I took my other hand and started jacking my dick. I no longer cared. It was dark and everyone else on the plane was still asleep. It felt so good, shawty breathing in my ear, I'm still fingering my girl, shawty massaging my girl's breast and I was choking the hell out of my dick. It was time for my girl to nut. Shawty needed to move just in case my girl wanted to magically wake up afterward. My girl squirmed around in her seat and I can feel her climax on my finger. She took her hand and placed it on my thigh. Yes, she was about to finish me off now, so shawty really needed to leave. My girl reached past me and put her hand underneath the shawty dress. I looked over and her eyes were still closed. I was fucked up. She knew the whole time. My girl finished shawty off and this trip easily became my favorite trip ever.

Sexy-Nine

You have made it to the end of "Sex Education- Written by a Black Woman." By this time, if you've read this book alone or with your partner, you should be ready to explore some sex in real life. It would be Re-DICK-ulous if you didn't think of the freaky or non-freaky stuff you wanted to do while reading. There really is no wrong way to have sex. Like I've said countless times, it all depends on what satisfies you and your partner. I feel like that's where the biggest problem comes. Couples don't discuss what they like and what they don't like, and most people don't believe that they have room to improve. Sorry to break it down to you, but your sex is wack to someone! To be honest, one will never know everything about sex. Every sex partner could have different sexual desires and ways to be pleased. Once you are really stuck with the person you will be with for the rest of your life, if that's the goal, then spice it up and keep the sex life healthy and fun.

The last activity involves some hands on experience. Have fun and let what you've learned or what you have known take you on a sex high!

Instruction-Cut out 12 pieces of paper.
Number them from 1-12 and place inside a cup
Each person pulls a number for a new position
Have Fun!

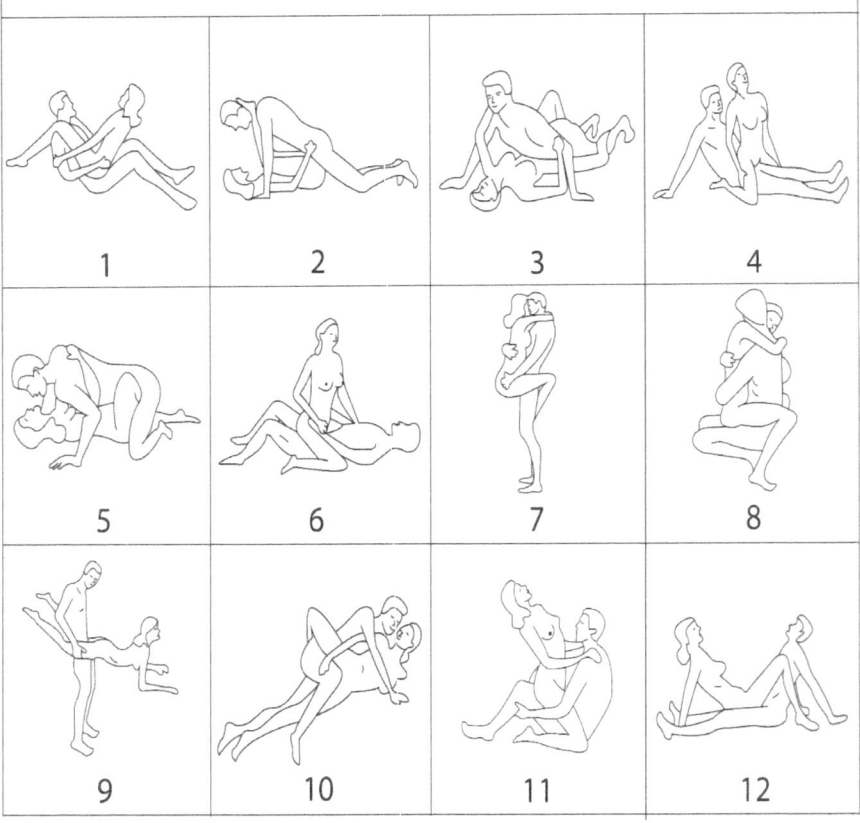

www.ingramcontent.com/pod-product-compliance
Lightning Source LLC
Chambersburg PA
CBHW050828180626
46814CB00004B/1509